The Invisible Victim

Written by Coleen Liebsch
Edited by Deborah Merkwan
Cover Art by Rudakata

Copyright 2020 PS Publishing
All Rights Reserved. Printed in the USA.

No part of this book may be reproduced or copied in any form without express written permission from the publisher.
ISBN: 978-1-942333-21-0

10 9 8 7 6 5 4 3 2

Thank you to the 2019/20 Middle-
School Students at Arlington and
Trinity Lutheran Aberdeen in SD.

Your input as beta readers was
invaluable to the final story of
"Invisible Victim."
Thank you for your enthusiasm and
contributions.

I hope you love the final story!
~Coleen

The Invisible Victim
By Coleen Liebsch

Chapter One

Caitlyn sat down at her computer and logged into Chatbook. She had shared a post at lunch and couldn't resist checking the number of "likes" she had received. The post was announcing the results of cheerleading tryouts, and Caitlyn had been selected for the squad… again.

The school's original post received 150 likes, but Caitlyn's shared message had over 570!

She was nearing the end of her sophomore year, and for all intents and purposes, Caitlyn and her group of friends ruled Jackson High. She scrolled through messages of congratulations and smiled to herself.

"You totally deserve it, Caitlyn! You're the best!!"

"You rock! Come over Friday night for a party to celebrate."

Comment after comment offered congratulations and admiration, until Caitlyn came across one that took her breath away.

"Fans aren't friends, you know."

Caitlyn's heart skipped a beat as she looked at the user-name, "Beccs." *Who in the world was Beccs?* Cailyn wondered to herself.

She'd heard about cyber-bullying, of course, but never experienced any kind of bullying herself. Everyone loved her! Why didn't this person? Was this the kind of thing advertisements warned about? As she thought about what the comment might mean, Caitlyn clicked on the user profile of "Beccs" to see if she could figure out who the person was.

As her computer took what felt like forever to bring up her unknown nemesis's page, Caitlyn tapped her fingers on the mousepad. She was so engrossed in reading she had no idea someone was sneaking up behind her.

"Boo!"

Caitlyn's heart nearly jumped out of her chest.

"Marshall!" She turned to see her younger brother backing away from her chair, smiling his gotcha smile. "I just about died! You scared me so much! If you weren't my baby brother, I swear…," She reached back to her keyboard and clicked the back button. In the event the mystery "Beccs'" page included any other negative information about her, Caitlyn didn't want her baby brother to see it. The screen returned to her cheerleading post.

"Ok, ok, don't swear." Marshall raised his hands in surrender. "You just seemed so into your computer screen I couldn't resist scaring you," he confessed. "I'm sorry."

"You're gonna be sorry when I pay you back for it. You just wait. When you least expect it… expect it." Caitlyn tried to sound ominous, but she could never stay mad at Marshall. She'd been wrapped around his finger since the moment he was born.

Caitlyn was four when her father took her to the hospital to meet her new baby brother. He was so tiny, no bigger than the baby doll she carried with her everywhere. She couldn't carry baby Marshall, but sometimes when she was very good, her mother would let her hold him carefully in the chair.

"So, what are you doing, checking on all your admirers?" Marshall asked as he peeked around her shoulder at the screen.

"No, I just thought I'd see if you had any yet." Caitlyn turned back to her screen and pretended to type. "Nope. None yet." She turned back around and smiled at her little brother. "Are Mom or Dad home yet?"

"No, they're at a meeting. It's just you and me tonight. Can we order pizza?" It didn't matter if their parents were at a meeting or in the living room, when it came close to dinner time, Marshall always asked if they could order pizza. This was one night he wouldn't be disappointed.

"Okay, what do you want on it?" Caitlyn asked nonchalantly.

"Really? Do you have money to pay for it? Really? This is so awesome! We never get to order pizza! Can we get a Supreme with everything on it?" Marshall was practically jumping out of his skin.

"We can get whatever you want." Caitlyn smiled at her little brother. "I might not even make Mom pay me back." She looked away, crinkled her nose, then looked back at Marshall. "Nah." They giggled together the way they only did when their parents weren't around.

"So how many likes does your post have now?" Marshall asked.

Caitlyn turned back to her computer screen and hit refresh. "It just passed 600. Isn't it weird how the school's post has so few likes and mine has so many?"

"It's not weird," Marshall said. "Everyone at school loves you. Everyone everywhere loves you. That's what I came to ask you about. You have to teach me how to fit in at middle school."

"I have to think back. That's been a long time ago now." Caitlyn sat back and rubbed her chin as all great philosophers do. She whistled her s's in her best old man voice. "Now when I was your age, you could get a candy bar for a quarter, you could."

"I'm serious, Caitlyn! Making friends comes easy for you, but I've never had to make a friend in my life. If you're just going to make fun of me, I don't even want to talk to you about it." Marshall stood up from his seat.

"Okay, okay, I was just kidding around. It helped for me to get involved in activities and sports. That's where you really get to know people."

"But I'm not good at anything," Marshall said sounding defeated.

"Are you kidding me? You're the best brother that has ever existed!" Caitlyn stood up and had Marshall in a headlock before he knew it. She ruffled his hair lightly, then set him free. "You are great at lots of things. Why did you quit playing soccer?" Caitlyn asked.

"The coach only cared about his favorites. If you weren't one of his pets, you didn't have any chance of playing. It just seemed stupid to waste my time practicing," Marshall answered. "There are a couple of clubs I might be interested in joining. I don't know. I wish there was a club for video games. I'd join that for sure."

"Yeah, I bet you would. Let's go order that pizza, and maybe I'll play a couple of rounds with you."

Caitlyn wasn't a huge fan of video games, but she was a very big fan of her little brother. She could suffer through his games to spend time with him. Besides, it would help her forget "Beccs" ever existed.

The only game Caitlyn ever played on her own was a game rated "mature," that required players to escape from rooms in a castle before the psychotic owner found and murdered them.

Marshall had never even been allowed to watch Caitlyn play the game, but she did owe him a scare.

As the game loaded, Marshall's heart continued to beat faster until the most graphic image he had ever seen burst onto the screen!

Chapter 2

"Ok, Marshall, are you sure you're ready for this?" Caitlyn asked.

"Oh yeah," Marshall replied, barely able to stay in his seat from excitement.

"The first room we're going to start out in is a guest bedroom. Speed up, buddy! You have to go as fast as you can through the entrance, so he doesn't see you," Caitlyn instructed.

They were both leaning forward as if to rush the avatar on the screen along. When Marshall finally made it through the entrance unscathed, the screen went dark.

"Is he going to come up behind us?" Marshall was already full of adrenaline.

"No, this is just a transition screen. It's going to open into a room that is really plain, like a cellar. What you have to do is figure out how to get out of it," Caitlyn coached.

"But you've done this room before, so you'll tell me how to get out, right?" Marshall tried to keep his nerves from showing in his voice.

"If you need it. Let's see if you can figure it out for yourself first."

The screen faded in from black and revealed a room exactly like Caitlyn had described. The walls seemed to be made of blocks of mud and there was only one door. In the center of the room was a table holding a newspaper and set of chop sticks.

Marshall immediately went to the door to see if it would open. It was locked. He looked around the room to see if there could be another way out. "The walls! I can use one of the chopsticks to dig a hole through the wall!"

Marshall proceeded to break the set of chopsticks and use one to start digging a hole in one of the sod blocks. It was working, but the dirt was hard packed and difficult to get through.

"Do you see the time clock on the corner of the screen?" Caitlyn asked. "That's how long you have until the owner of the house finds you. Right now you have about five minutes to get out of this room."

Marshall's heart beat frantically as his head searched for ways to get out of the room. "Newspaper," he muttered. "What could I use a newspaper for?" He thought for a good thirty seconds before Caitlyn again freaked him out by announcing the time.

"Why don't you look through the keyhole of the door and see if you can see anything in the hallway," Caitlyn prompted.

Marshall used his controller to position his character at the door. When his view changed to the keyhole itself, he could see the key was stuck in the door. Excitement spread through his body. He had the solution!

He pulled the chopsticks out and tried to maneuver them into the keyhole. "If I can just get these positioned right… I think I can turn that key." Marshal's tongue was hanging out of the right side of his mouth just a bit.

Caitlyn smiled as she looked at her little brother. He always bit his tongue when he was concentrating. She wondered how much she should help him as the time ticked away.

It wasn't long before Marshall realized he couldn't fit both chopsticks in the keyhole at the same time. He sat down hard on his chair in frustration.

"Ok, don't worry. I'll help you." Caitlyn could see the stress was getting to her baby brother. "What if you use one of the chopsticks to push the key out of the hole?" she asked.

"Well, all that's going to do is drop it on the ground. How would I reach under the door?" Marshall asked.

"What else is in the room?" Caitlyn asked calmly, but Marshall's anxiety was increasing as he glanced at the clock and saw one minute.

"The newspaper is all I've got! What am I supposed to do with a newspaper?" Marshall asked a little too loudly. "Maybe if it was the next day's paper I could read about how this guy murders me in fifty seconds! How do I get out of this room?"

"Ok, ok, if you push the newspaper under the door, then push the key out with the chopstick it will fall on the newspaper." Caitlyn was speaking far too slowly for Marshall's comfort.

"So? What difference is that going to make? I'm down to 30 seconds and I... oh..." Marshall finally understood. He moved his avatar to the table to collect the newspaper, then went to the door to slide it under. Just as he pushed the newspaper under the door, Caitlyn chimed in.

"You picked up one of the chopsticks too, didn't you?"

"Oh crap, no! I've got to go back to the table!"

"Hurry up, Marshall. You're down to 20 seconds, and you're still going to have to unlock the door."

"I'm hurrying, I'm hurrying! Ok. I've got the chopstick. Keep telling me the time!"

By the time Marshall had the chopstick stuck into the keyhole the time was down to ten seconds. Caitlyn started counting backwards to the moment of no escape. Just as Caitlyn reached zero, Marshall unlocked the door and swung it open.

Standing center screen was the most terrifying character Marshall had ever seen in a video game. The owner of the mansion, insane to the point of looking inhuman, stood before him holding an axe.

Terror froze Marshall in place, but it wouldn't have mattered. Within a fraction of a second the character raised the axe above his head and brought it down squarely on his target. What followed was far more graphic than Marshall had ever imaged the game being.

"Oh man, you almost made it!" Caitlyn laughed as she looked over at her brother's face. It was whiter than it was when he had the flu. "Are you ok, Dude?" she asked.

"Yeah," Marshall answered shakily. "I'm ok. That was a crazy game, though!"

His color had barely started to return to normal before he was begging to play again. Caitlyn was just about to push "Play Again," when they heard the front door open.

"We're home!" The kids heard the front door close as Caitlyn switched over to Marshall's racing game.

"Grand Champion of the World, right here." Caitlyn fist pumped the air as if she were holding a trophy. "Hi Mom, hi Dad," she said casually. She looked over at Marshall to make sure he was truly recovered.

Marshall set down his controller as their parents came into the room. "Yeah, she beat me again. How was the meeting?" he asked.

"It was good. Long, but good," their mother Janis answered. "Did you both get something to eat?"

"We ordered pizza. The receipt is on the counter for you," Caitlyn smiled. "We have some left over if you guys are still hungry."

"Thanks, honey, but we had a big dinner at the meeting," Janis answered as she took off her coat.

Their father Kyle felt differently. "I'd try a piece," he said as he reached into the box for a slice. "What are you playing?"

"The Car Race," Marshall answered. "Do you want to play?"

"I'd love to, Marsh, but I still have some work to get done tonight. Thanks for the pizza, though." Kyle kissed the heads of both his children, then nibbled on pizza as he left the room.

"Do you want to play, Mom?" Marshall asked.

"Oh no, honey. Thank you for asking, but I'd rather watch you two play. I'm going to sort pictures and watch." She pulled out a box of loose photographs from under the couch, and both kids groaned. Janis had been sorting pictures for as long as either of them could remember. They had bought her a digital camera and a digital photo frame for Mother's Day, but she still wanted everything printed out. She preferred having an actual photo to hold.

"It's hard to believe there are only two months left of school," Janis began. "Have either of you thought about what you want to do this summer?"

"The Aqua Center called to ask if I would lifeguard again this summer. I want to do that for sure, but I was thinking about getting a second job, too," Caitlyn answered.

"I don't know what I'm going to do yet," Marshall said. "I was thinking about asking if anyone in the neighborhood would want me to mow their lawns."

"I think that's a great idea, honey!" Janis replied. "It would be wonderful for you to spend more time outside this summer. We certainly have all the equipment you would need. I'm sure Dad would be happy to help you haul the mower on the trailer. Let's talk to him about it when he finishes working."

The rest of the evening went on as most evenings in the Johnson household do. Janis and the kids talked about their days, things they needed for school, and the days they would need sack lunches.

Kyle found more work than he'd expected when he logged onto his computer and wound up working the rest of the evening. By 10:30, Janis and the kids were ready for bed.

"Don't forget to brush your teeth!" Janis reminded from the bottom of the stairway.

"We know," Caitlyn and Marshall replied in unison.

"Do we ever forget to brush our teeth?" Caitlyn asked Marshall while foaming at the mouth with toothpaste. They were standing side by side at the "his and her" sinks in their bathroom.

The sibling's bedrooms were separated by a "Jack and Jill" bathroom that had two sinks in the washroom. The toilet and shower were in a smaller attached room for privacy.

"Oh yeah," Marshall answered. "I forget all the time. Sometimes I don't even forget, I just pretend to forget so I don't have to do it."

Caitlyn spit into the sink and rinsed her mouth. "Yeah, well, you're going to be sorry when your teeth rot out of your head, you goofball," she teased. "Sleep well, Bud. I'll see you in the morning."

"Goodnight, Caity," Marshall answered as he closed the door to his bedroom.

Spending time with Marshall had almost made Caitlyn forget about the nasty comment on her post. Almost.

Chapter Three

"Good Morning." Janis greeted both children at the bottom of the stairs. They were drawn down by the smell of pancakes and bacon. "I felt so bad about leaving you alone for dinner last night that I made a big breakfast. Grab a plate, and fill 'er up," Janis commanded. "Is there anything exciting going on in school today for either of you?"

"Not really," Caitlyn answered as Marshall said, "No," at the same time.

"You've got end-of-year tests coming up pretty soon. Do you feel like you're ready for them?"

Marshall blew milk out of his mouth to demonstrate how ludicrous his mother's question was.

"Gross! Mom, why does he have to do things like that? Marshall Allen Langston, you are going to clean that up right now." Caitlyn pushed the napkin holder toward her brother. "You got milk all over me, you pig."

"Totally worth it," Marshall said softly through his smile.

"Are you going to act that way when you get to middle school next year, young man?" Janis asked Marshall as he wiped up the table. "Don't forget to use a wet rag first, so the table isn't sticky when you're finished. It sounds like you'd better make some time in your evenings for studying, my dear boy."

"We still have three weeks before tests start. If I started studying now, I wouldn't remember it when test time got here," Marshall argued. "They haven't even given us our study guides yet."

"You know, they're not going to give you study guides in middle school," Caitlyn told her brother. "You're going to have to learn how to make your own."

"Middle school just keeps sounding better and better," Marshall groaned. His elation over his spit milk was fading fast.

"Are you worried about going to a new school next year? There will be a lot of kids you know there," Janis said.

"I know, but Jacob and Elliott are going to private school, and Sean isn't going to be in my section. It doesn't even sound like we have a single class together during the day. There are going to be six hundred seventh graders, and the only one I'm really friends with I'm never gonna see." Marshall took a deep breath. "I guess I'm kinda nervous about it."

"Well, don't worry, little brother. I have some friends with brothers and sisters who go to school at Wilmont. I'll put in a good word for you." Caitlyn winked in reassurance.

Caitlyn's influence would make a difference with a few people at the school, but she would be attending Lincoln High. Even if she convinced her friends to make their siblings talk to him, it would only last for one conversation. It would be up to him to win them over from there, and he wasn't good at that. She wouldn't be there to make people be nice to him.

Life was perfect for Marshall up until second grade. He and Caitlyn went to the same school, so she had won everyone over before he even started school. Marshall was more than happy to live in her shadow. He may not have been as loved as his sister, but he certainly felt popular. Other students were always seeking him out to ask how his sister was doing and what she had been up to lately. Marshall's link to popularity faded over the years since Caity moved on, but it still helped with the teachers. What if he didn't have any of the same teachers his sister had at the middle school? Who would he be without his sister?

"Good morning, Family." Kyle walked into the kitchen straightening his tie and immediately went to Janis to kiss her good morning. "Breakfast smells delicious. What's the occasion?"

"I felt bad we were gone so long last night, so I wanted to do something special this morning," Janis replied as she handed him a plate.

"Breakfast AND paying me back for the pizza last night." Caitlyn smiled. "Now that's a great way to start the day." She stabbed a piece of pancake and put it in her mouth.

"Very subtle, my dear." Janis rolled her eyes as she reached across the counter for her purse. "What's on your agenda today, Kyle?"

"Meetings all day. My last one starts at 5:00, so I don't know what time I'll wind up getting home tonight."

"Well, you look great, so I'm sure they will all go wonderfully. I'll plan dinner for around seven but send me a text if you'll be later than that." She placed a pancake on a plate and cut it into bite-sized pieces, then ate standing up.

"Caitlyn, you're picking Marshall up after band practice this afternoon, right?" Janis asked.

"Yes, 4:30 at the auditorium, right?"

"Yeah," Marshall sounded like he would rather be sleeping. "Pick me up at door two, though. There's less of a line there."

With the pancakes devoured and the day's plans finalized, Caitlyn and Marshall left for school as Janis cleaned up the breakfast dishes. Her thoughts drifted to her big-hearted son who worried too much about what others thought of him.

Chapter Four

Marshall sat at the table he always sat at with his friends for lunch and waited for them to join him. *This is what it's going to be like next year. I'll be sitting at a table all by myself, but no one else will be coming to eat with me,* he thought to himself. Just then, Jacob and Sean plopped down on each side of him.

"What's up, Buttercup? You're having the meatloaf? Puke! I'm having a hamburger... at least I know what's in that," Sean said.

"Do you really?" Marshall raised one eyebrow in an ominous look. "Do you really know what's in that hamburger? Mwah, ha, ha."

"You're both morons," Jacob said. "Have either of you started studying yet? Maybe we should do, like a study group or something."

At that moment, Elliott sat down next to Sean at the round lunch table. "What are you guys talking about?"

"Jacob thinks we should form a study group because we're morons," Marshall answered.

"Isn't a test supposed to be about what we learned from the teacher? If I study, then that's just gonna show what I taught myself," Sean said. The boys all laughed.

"We could get together at my house to study," Elliott volunteered. "I can ask Mom if this weekend would work."

The boys made small talk as they ate their lunch, then Marshall brought up the subject they rarely discussed.

"Are you guys worried about going off to middle school next year?" Marshall spoke softly.

"Heck no!" Jacob answered. "I'm going to be the coolest kid at prep school."

"You're forgetting I'll be there too," Elliott reminded.

"No, I'm not." Jacob said as he forked a piece of meatloaf into his mouth.

"At least Sean and I will be able to see each other at lunch time," Marshall interjected.

"No, we won't," Sean said through a mouthful of hamburger. "The different sections go to lunch at different times, so the cafeteria doesn't get too crowded. We don't even have the same hallways, so we'll only see each other before and after school."

"You know, one good thing about going somewhere that nobody knows us is that we can turn into anybody we want to be," Jacob said.

"What are you talking about?" Elliott asked. "You gonna change your name at prep school or something?"

"No, I just mean nobody knows that Marshall blew a snot bubble in second grade when he had that cold. Nobody knows that I peed my pants in third grade because you jerk wads made me laugh so hard. For all they know, we could have been the coolest kids in elementary," Jacob explained.

"Interesting. Anyone we want to be, huh?" Marshall said under his breath. The rest of the guys pondered their own thoughts about the new possibilities before them.

They explored the options of becoming super-heroes, street-studs, and brainiacs. Then one by one, the guys became lost in their own thoughts, until...

"You know, Ava will be going to our middle school, Marshall." The sing-song-y way Sean said it made it clear what he was implying.

"She's just a friend. I don't even think of her that way. She's just a great person to talk to when you dorks aren't around."

Marshall had been defending his friendship with Ava for two years. The truth was, he enjoyed talking with her. Most of the time they talked about the makeup she just bought or the clothes that were in style, but she gave such a different perspective from his male friends. He liked that.

He always lied about how much he talked to her, though. His friends would tease him to death if they knew she called him at least once a week. No one knew that he talked to Ava every week, not even his sister.

Chapter Five

Caitlyn took a bite of her salad as another person squished onto a seat at their cafeteria table. It was already full to the point people were sharing seats, but that wasn't anything unusual. Caitlyn and her group of friends were the most popular girls in school.

There were six seats at the round table, which was perfect for Caitlyn's group. The kids squishing in were usually boys asking for dates or girls looking for a reason to talk to someone in the group. The newest addition to the table was a girl none of them liked very much.

Marsha always tried just a little too hard to fit into a group. She asked for more details about things that were none of her business, when people weren't even talking to her. In fact, eavesdropping was the only way Marsha ever learned about social happenings. She invited herself to events she over-heard people talking about, and she never knew when to leave.

As Marsha sat down on the edge of Sarah's seat, you could almost hear the girls' eyes roll. Fortunately, she was looking down to make sure her butt would fit on the seat and didn't see them.

"Greetings, ladies," Marsha said as she opened her milk carton. Since the table had stopped talking as soon as she sat down, it made for an easy opening for her. "What are you all up to?"

"Not all that much, Marsha. We were just talking about how much we needed to study for tests. What's new with you?" Rebecca asked. Rebecca was by far the nicest of Caitlyn's friends. She tried to include everyone whether she liked them or not.

"I'm just enjoying this meatloaf with friends," Marsha said. When no one responded, she added: "End-of-year tests are going to suck. Does anyone want to study together?"

Simultaneously, each of the girls started giving reasons why she was already committed. In some cases, they pointed to others in the group; in other cases, they said they studied better alone. At the end of the conversation, Marsha hadn't received a glimmer of interest, not even from Rebecca.

"I guess with the study guide it's not like we can't quiz ourselves, right?" Marsha asked rhetorically.

Conversations that left Marsha out sprung up in small pockets around the table. They talked about the end-of-year dance. They talked about their boyfriends. They talked about everything except plans where Marsha could include herself. They had all learned that lesson the hard way.

None of them wanted Marsha around. It wasn't because there was anything wrong with her per se. She just tried too hard to make friends. In high school, that was social suicide.

"Was there anything else you wanted to talk to us about?" Caitlyn asked Marsha.

"No, not really. I was just wondering what everyone was up to," Marsha answered, tilting her head to the side as if she didn't understand why the question was asked.

"We don't want to keep you from your friends, then." Caitlyn smiled her photo-perfect smile at Marsha. "It looks like Sarah is about ready to fall off the seat, but it was good seeing you." And with that, Marsha knew she was dismissed.

Marsha gathered her tray with her head down and gave a tiny wave with her fingers as she stood up to leave.

The other girls at the table snickered behind their hands, but Caitlyn kept perfect composure the entire time. "Sometimes you've got to be cruel to be kind, ladies."

"How can Marsha be so completely oblivious to the fact that no one wants her around?" Pam asked no one in particular.

"Maybe she's just so used to being unwanted that it doesn't even phase her," Rebecca answered.

With their interloper out of the picture, the girls went back to discussing plans for forming a study group. More importantly, they went back to talking about Caitlyn's post and the mystery comment.

"I just don't understand what that's supposed to mean, 'Fans aren't friends.' Is that supposed to mean I don't have any real friends or something?" Caitlyn looked around at the girls she had considered as close as sisters since elementary school. "And who the hell is 'Beccs?'"

"Did it show how long you'd been friends with the person, or did you look at the profile to see if she looked familiar?" Rebecca asked.

"No," Caitlyn answered in a voice much quieter than her normal. "I was going to, but then my stupid computer was too slow. I'll look the wench up when I get home from school."

Andromeda piped in, "I know the picture on the comment is small, but didn't the profile picture look familiar? Do you have any mutual friends or anything?"

"I don't know. It took so long to pull her profile up I didn't even get a chance to see those things."

Caitlyn looked down at her plate and missed the exchange of looks between her closest friends.

After a nudge from Pam, Rebecca spoke up. "Maybe the comment means that sometimes you worry more about what people you barely know think of you than you do what's going on with your real friends."

"What? Are you serious? You all know how much you mean to me. You're my best friends, for crying out loud. That can't be it." Caitlyn said as the bell signifying the end of lunch rang through the cafeteria.

Chapter Six

Caitlyn waited in the parking lot of Marshall's school for him to come out. It was a beautiful day, and she had the top down on her convertible. She leaned her head back in the seat and turned the radio up just a little bit higher. Her favorite song was playing, and she was allowing the warmth of the sun to melt away her thoughts about what Rebecca had said.

"Well, hi!" An irritating voice rang in her left ear over the sound of a new engine pulling up. Caitlyn raised her head to see it was Marsha.

"I didn't know you had to come here after school too. We should car-pool some time," Marsha said cheerfully. She was always cheerful. That was one of the things that annoyed Caitlyn the most about her. It didn't matter what you said or did, Marsha never got the hint she wasn't wanted.

Caitlyn lifted her sunglasses and turned her head in the direction of the truck that had pulled up on her left.

"Hello, Marsha," Caitlyn replied coldly. She put her sunglasses back in place and leaned her head back on the seat. Perhaps pretending Marsha was invisible would be the way to get rid of her.

"What's that song you're listening to?" Marsha had to yell a little louder to be heard, as she leaned a further toward her passenger window.

Caitlyn turned the volume of her radio louder and ignored Marsha completely. As the song was ending, she saw her little brother running out of the building. A few seconds later children were running every direction to parked cars. Marshall spotted his sister immediately.

"Alright! We're gonna get to drive with the top down!" Marshall threw his backpack behind the passenger seat and climbed into his sister's car. She turned the stereo down to almost zero. Marshall fastened his seat belt with one arm as he pulled the door closed with the other. "How was your day?" he asked.

Before his sister could answer, they were interrupted.

"See you later, Caitlyn." Marsha's sister had climbed into her truck and they were pulling away. Caitlyn waved her hand in Marsha's general direction in a way that was more dismissive than friendly.

"Who's that?" Marshall asked.

"Nobody. Just some invisible who can't take a hint. My day was alright. How was yours?" It didn't matter how many problems Caitlyn had on her mind. She would never put them on her brother. She was far too protective to hurt him, even indirectly.

"It was alright. I got a ton of homework, though. I don't get what integers are. I tried to ask the teacher, but he just said, 'Everyone else understands it.' I hate math."

"Don't worry, Bud. I can help you with it. I wish Mrs. Melner was still teaching math. She was great at explaining everything. We'll work on it tonight. What else happened?"

"The guys and I are going to do a study group. I'm hopin' everybody studies ahead of time so we can just play video games. That's what I'm gonna do," Marshal said.

"You and your video games. What do you get out of them?" Caitlyn asked as she pulled the car out of the school parking lot. "I mean, I like playing sometimes too, but it's not an obsession for me."

"What about Chatbook? You spend more time on there than I do on video games," Marshall said.

Caitlyn thought of "Becc's" comments and found it harder to maintain her cheerful façade. "That's different. That's socializing. If I have a problem with homework, I ask someone on Chatbook. If I want to find out what's going on this weekend, I look on Chatbook. It's like talking to all of my friends on the phone at once," Caitlyn defended.

"Well, maybe I'll get on Chatbook and see what all the fuss is about," Marshall said.

"You're too young," Caitlyn replied immediately.

"How old do you have to be?"

"Well, technically you're supposed to be 18," Caitlyn answered.

"You're not 18. How did you get an account?" Marshall asked.

"I just added a few years to my birthday. It thinks I'm 24 now," Caitlyn giggled. "But that's different. You're not ready to get on there. I think you should wait until you're at least a freshman."

"Video games are more fun, anyway. Besides, I talk to my friends on there all the time. I can even talk to Edward, and he moved away four years ago. We play games together all the time," Marshall said.

"How is Edward doing?" Caitlyn asked. Before he moved across the country, he spent almost every day at our house. "I miss him."

"He's good. His sisters still bug him, but other than that he's good," Marshall replied.

They spent the rest of the drive talking about friends and tests. They arrived at the house at the same time as their mother. Caitlyn pulled her car into the garage and turned off the engine. Their mother pulled the car into the adjoining stall and did the same. They all opened their car doors simultaneously.

"Hi guys. How was school today?" Janis asked.

"It was okay. How was your day?" Caitlyn answered.

"It was tremendous! I sold the house on First Street, and I'm pretty sure I'll have an offer on Ventura by morning." Janis was beaming. "I thought we would have a celebration dinner tonight. What sounds good to you two?"

"Pizza!" Marshall yelled, as Caitlyn replied, "Tacos."

"Pizza and tacos, it is," Janis announced as she laughed at her children's predictability.

Chapter Seven

Marshall couldn't get the thought of re-inventing himself out of his head. The fears he had at the thought of being without his friends turned to excitement. Who was he without his friends? Who was he without the influence of his sister?

The only person who knew the real him was Ava. He would never admit it to any of the guys, but Ava was his best friend. She was the one who heard his inner-most thoughts, and he was the one who heard hers.

Ava lived in a household very, different from Marshall's. Her parents were hippies in every sense of the word. They not only accepted Ava's need for experimentation, they encouraged it.

Ava was a year older than Marshall, and on her thirteenth birthday she confessed to him that she was bi-sexual. Marshall had asked a billion questions about how she knew who she liked best when she'd never dated anyone before. Had she told her parents? Did anyone else know?

In the end, no one knew except Marshall. Ava wasn't a popular student, and she wasn't involved in activities. No one cared what she did or didn't do at her school. She was an invisible. Having

Marshall to talk with made things easier, but her sexuality wasn't the only thing she questioned.

"I know it seems like it's great to have parents who let you do anything, but I feel like they don't even care what I do," Ava told Marshall on the phone. "If I get an F, they sign my report card and say nothing. If I get an A+... same thing. If I stay out until midnight on a school night, they don't even say anything. Sometimes I feel like they don't care whether I'm dead or alive."

Marshall never knew what to say when Ava talked about her parents. He couldn't imagine having parents that let him do whatever he wanted. He couldn't imagine having parents who wouldn't lose their minds if he brought home a report card with an F on it!

"Wouldn't it be great if we could mash our parents together? If we could take your parents' 'Who cares' philosophy and my parents' 'We must know everything you do' philosophy, we'd probably both have perfect families," Marshall said.

"Oh, please, your family IS perfect," Ava said. "I've never even met them in person, but I know they care about everything you do."

"Having to be perfect isn't great either, you know," Marshall said. "You think it's easy to have parents who watch everything you do? The only place I ever get away from them is in my bedroom. If I don't have A's, I have to explain it. If I want to quit a group, I have to hear about how it could benefit me in my future. Nothing is ever about who I want to be. It's always about who they want me to be." Then Marshall added much quieter, "If they knew the real me, they'd probably hate me. I don't care about getting into the best schools. I don't care about being in the right groups. At least your parents accept you for who you are, regardless of who that is."

"Yeah, I suppose that's true. Still, it would be nice if they could just both be a little more like the other," Ava said.

"I definitely agree with that," Marshall replied. "So, how are things going with Maria?"

"Awful. She doesn't want to be friends anymore since she found out I was bi." Ava sounded sad. "We've been friends since second grade, but now she doesn't want to hang out with me because people will think she's a lesbian."

"Aw geez, I'm sorry, Ava. She'll come around. She just needs some time."

"That's what my mom said, but I don't think so. She pretends like I'm invisible when we see each other in the hallway at school," Ava said. "When everyone found out she had lice in third grade, I was the one who stood by her. I even said it could happen to anyone. I didn't care that it hurt my own reputation. She was my friend. Then when it comes time for her to defend me, nope. I'm not any different than I was six months ago when she cried on my shoulder because Josh dumped her. I don't even see her like that, geez!"

"Has she talked to you at all?" Marshall asked.

"Not really. She bumped into me in the hallway one day and said, 'Excuse me,' but that's all she's said to me since I came out," Ava answered. "I tried calling her a couple of times, but it went straight to voicemail. She's got me blocked. She un-friended me on Chatbook, too, so I don't even know what she's saying about me."

"You're on Chatbook?" Marshall asked.

"Yeah, I've been on there since I was ten," Ava said. "I've got about 200 friends, but most of them are people I don't really know. There isn't anyone I could ask to troll her and see what she's saying about me. Hey, maybe your sister. Do you think your sister would do it?"

"I don't know," Marshall said. "I'll ask her and give you a call back." He ended the call and yelled for his sister. A few minutes later, Caitlyn poked her head in his door.

"Would you do me a Chatbook favor?" Marshall asked.

"Why do I think I should sit down for this?" Caitlyn asked as she moved to sit on his bed.

"Well, Ava's friend is mad at her and blocked her on everything. She's wondering if she's saying bad things about her on-line. Could you troll her?"

"Oh sure. Just have Ava send me a friend request, then she can send me a link to the person she wants me to check out." Caitlyn stood to leave. "I can always use another friend." She winked at her little brother as she walked out of the room.

Marshall called Ava back to let her know Caity was willing to help.

Chapter Eight

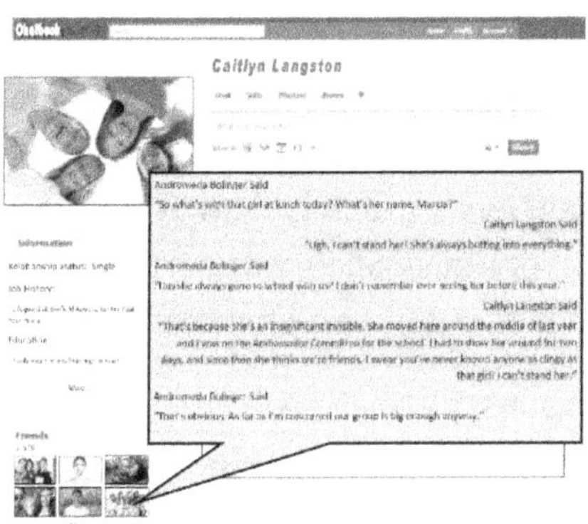

Caitlyn logged onto Chatbook and saw a message from her friend Andromeda.

"So, what's with that girl at lunch today? What's her name, Marsha?" Andromeda's message read.

Caitlyn replied, "Ugh, I can't stand her! She's always butting into everything."

Andromeda typed back, "Has she always gone to school with us? I don't remember ever seeing her before this year."

"That's because she's an insignificant invisible," Caitlyn typed in response. "She moved here around the middle of last year when I was on the Ambassador Committee for the school. I had to show her around for two days, and since then she thinks we're best friends. I swear you've never known anyone as clingy as that girl! I can't stand her."

"That's obvious," Andromeda replied. "As far as I'm concerned our group is big enough anyway."

"Agreed," Caitlyn said. "This is the first time I've logged in since lunch. I'm going to look up the profile of that 'Beccs' and check her out."

Andromeda began typing a message back, then the scrolling stopped. The scrolling started again on Caitlyn's screen showing Andromeda was typing a reply. As the profile belonging to "Beccs" pulled up on Caitlyn's screen, the scrolling from Andromeda stopped again.

Now it was Andromeda's turn to wait as Caitlyn typed a message into their chat screen.

"OMG! 'Beccs' is REBECCA!!!! WTF?" Caitlyn messaged.

Just as she hit send on her message, a new friend request popped up on her screen.

The friend request took over her message screen, and Caitlyn clicked on it as she waited for Andromeda to reply with her own shock at Rebecca's betrayal.

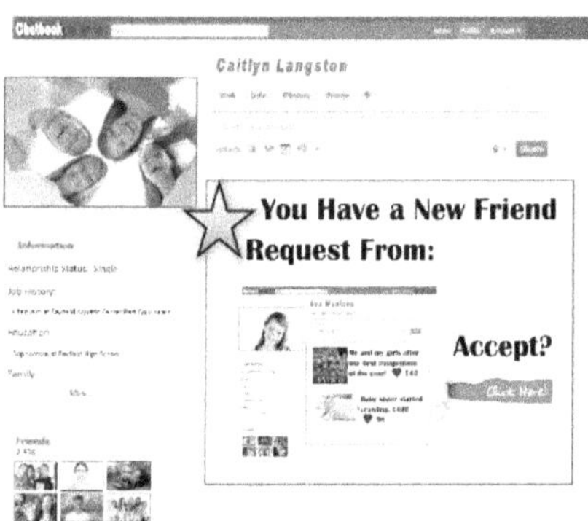

request came from Marshall's friend Ava, so Caitlyn accepted the invitation. She immediately saw that Ava was typing her a message, but her thoughts were still on "Beccs." It wasn't long before the message box popped up on her screen.

"Hi, Caitlyn. I am Ava. I am a friend of Marshall's. A girl in my school has been harassing me on-line for like 2 months. Could you check out her page and see if she's writing anything about me?"

"Sure! What's her name?" Caitlyn asked as her mind was raced with thoughts of Rebecca."

How was I supposed to know that Rebecca calls herself Beccs? It's not like any of the rest of us have ever called her that. And what does she mean by "fans aren't friends." Is that supposed to mean I'm some kind of terrible friend? If she has such a problem with me, then why wouldn't she have the guts to talk to me in person? If she says things like that on MY post, what is she saying about me behind my back?

At that moment, it occurred to Caitlyn that Andromeda was taking an especially long time to reply. *OMG,* she thought to herself. *Andromeda already KNEW it was Rebecca.*

While she was the best friend anyone could ever have if she liked you, Caitlyn could be downright meteoric if she didn't. As her feelings flashed between humiliation, anger, sadness, embarassment, frustration and back again, Caitlyn went in to defend Ava.

A message popped up on Caitlyn's screen: "Her name is Maria Salvadora. I'll send you a link to her page." And with that, Ava disappeared from the conversation for a moment. The next thing Caitlyn saw was a link to Maria's page.

When Caitlyn opened the link, she was stunned. Maria didn't just have a couple of posts bashing Ava, her entire page was dedicated to it!

Maria had pictures of Ava just waking up at a slumber party. Her hair was a mess and her makeup was smeared. The angle of the picture made it look like Maria was twice her size and the caption said, "Sad when people let themselves go this much." There were pictures of Ava ugly crying after her dog died. Posing without a shirt on and even sitting on the toilet. The worst part of every picture was the caption.

"Here's Ava living on the streets after she decides she's a lesbo." The picture had been taken on the day Ava had the flu and walked to urgent care.

"The first time Ava sold herself for money," was the caption across the picture of Ava ugly crying.

Caitlyn was sucked into the message boards of every entry as if they were things her own friends might have been saying about her. There were occasional comments of support, but only in the beginning. Anyone who stood up to support Ava was attacked just as viciously as the original post. Eventually, the comments of support stopped. That's when the posts became truly ugly.

"If you have PE with Ava, you'd better make sure you skip the shower! I don't care how old she is. She's a pedophile if I've ever seen one!"

"I have a friend who told me she was raped by Ava in the tunnel on the playground in fourth grade. She's still in therapy, so it's got to be true!"

"Has anyone checked the internet for the pervs in our area? Someone needs to see if Ava is on it. If she's not, she should be!"

The more support a negative post received, the more hateful the next became.

Caitlyn's heart beat a little faster. A surge of adreneline raced through her body at the thought of taking a punk "b" down... hard. She messaged Ava.

"Do you have any pictures of you and Maria hugging, kissing, wearing pajamas, or anything like that? The newer the better!" Caitlyn typed.

"I'll look back through my pictures...," Ava replied. Several moments passed before Caitlyn's computer pinged with a treasure trove of photos to choose from. Caitlyn laughed out loud at how easy it was going to be to turn the tables on Maria. She got to work creating the post.

"Oh my God," Ava typed. "I just saw your post on Maria's Chatbook page! And telling everyone to screenshot and re-post it rather than share it, was perfect! Now even if she deletes her posts it's going to stay out there. That was just brilliant! How did you ever think of something like that?"

Caitlyn thought about how much she wished she were sending the message to Rebecca. "Trade secrets, my dear. Look, the only reason she would be that upset about you being bi is because she was in love with you. I simply made a post that proved it."

"I just refreshed my page and your post has been liked 250 times already! I wonder how many of those people will re-post what you put up?" Ava messaged.

Before Caitlyn could type a reply, Ava was typing again.

"I just got an answer to my question! Maria just messaged me and said that over half the people she knows have un-friended her! She is blowing up my phone with apologies and questions. I'm not even going to reply☺ She can just feel as bad as she's been making me feel for a while. Thanks, Caitlyn! Marshall's right. You are the best! I totally owe you one!"

"No problem." Caitlyn replied, but a new wave of sadness washed over her mind. "Any friend of Marshall's…" she typed as she wondered whether she had any real friends.

Sadness turned to humiliation and anger again just as a new friend request popped up on her screen. Caitlyn opened the invitation and couldn't believe her eyes.

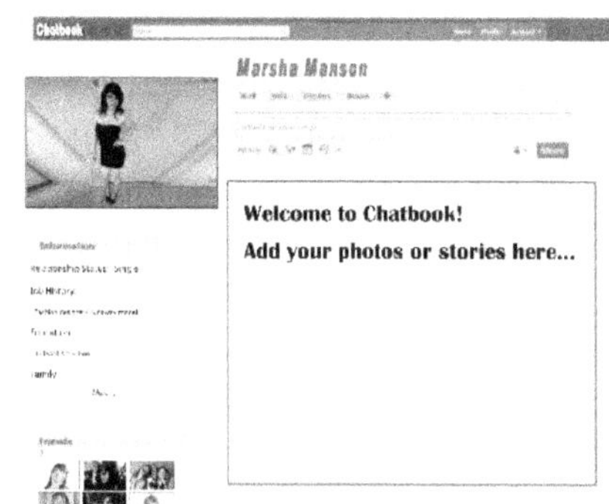

"You have got to be kidding me," she said out loud.

Chapter Nine

Marshall sat in his room thinking about the idea of becoming anyone he wanted to be. If it weren't for his friends, his family, or even his own belief system, who *would* he be? He thought back to the years when he and Caitlyn were both in elementary school.

He remembered watching his older sister with her friends on the playground. They would be jumping rope or practicing cheer-leading moves. It all seemed so easy. Marshall always had Elliott to play with, but what he really wanted to do was play with his sister and her friends.

Elliott lived next door, so they'd known each other since before either of them could remember. Their families' properties shared a back yard, and the kids met outside when their moms started visiting over the fence with their newborns. Elliott had a brother Caitlyn's age. When the kids got older, they started going outside to play together on their own.

Marshall was content sitting in the lookout tower of the swing set, watching his sister play with her friends. Elliott always had other ideas. It was Elliott who taught Marshall how to play football and soccer. It was Elliott who taught Marshall how to look cool on the school bus, but it was Caity whose approval mattered most.

Marshall's continued distraction as a playmate might have been why Elliott sought out the friendship of Sean on their first day of preschool. Being neighbors was likely what kept Marshall in the group of friends, because Sean and Elliott clearly had more in common. When Jacob moved to the school, he seemed to provide the link between interests the group needed. If nothing else, they could play board games that needed four players, even if they didn't always agree what game it should be.

It seemed to Marshall that everyone other than himself fit into some kind of "slot." There were the jocks and the cheerleaders. There were the smart kids and the druggies, but where did he fit in? Outside his own family, it seemed like nowhere. He had no idea what he wanted to be when he grew up. He had no idea if he ever wanted to get married. Marshall didn't even know if he liked girls, other than as friends, of course.

That wasn't something he could ever tell any of the guys. It was something only Ava knew. Ava knew all of Marshall's deepest secrets and greatest fears. She probably knew him better than he knew himself. She was the one who consoled him when Caitlyn's loser boyfriend told him to get lost for the first time. She was the one who celebrated with him when that loser boyfriend was kicked to the curb.

Dinner came and went in a blur as Marshall thought about his future and the potential it may or may not hold. He remembered his mother asking him why he was so distracted and his father talking about some work deal. Other than that, the conversations went on without him.

After dinner, Janis went to the kitchen to clean up as Kyle stood up to help her clear the table. They had been together long enough to work in rhythm most days.

Caitlyn had gone to her room to finish her homework. After that, she was going to log onto her Chatbook to help Ava.

With everyone else in the house occupied, Marshall decided to take a stab at re-inventing himself.

He went into his mother's closet and took one of the garment bags from the back of her rows of clothes. He found a wig that she had worn for Halloween once, then he grabbed a pair of shoes. Finally, Marshall went to the master bathroom to gather the rest of the things he would need. The household paid no attention when he closed and locked the door to his bedroom.

Chapter Ten

As Caitlyn looked at the profile picture attached to the friend request she'd just received, she crinkled her nose in disgust. What was it going to take for Marsha to get the message she didn't want to be friends?

Caitlyn accepted the request from Marsha and waited for the connection to be verified. As soon as it was, Caitlyn went out to the freshly created personal space on "Marsha's" page and started in.

"So, do you think just because you use some made-up profile picture I'm not gonna know who you are?" Caitlyn typed into the box.

"You mean you recognize me?" Marsha replied.

"Are you kidding? You think some whore-ish make-up and a stupid ass wig change who you are?" Caitlyn allowed all of the venom she felt toward her own friends into the message. She waited several seconds after her message was sent, but when there wasn't an indication Marsha was typing. Caitlyn started in again.

"People barely tolerate you, and it was only because I asked them to! You've been nothing but a pain in the ass, butting in everywhere you're not wanted."

The buffering symbol that showed the other person was typing a message spooled for about five seconds then stopped. Caitlyn watched it start up again and spin for about fifteen seconds before it stopped. She had left Marsha speechless and smiled at the idea of her former Ambassador pity project left with nothing to say.

"You obviously don't know how to stand in high heels and that dress looks like one my mother has! I'm embarrassed to have my other Chatbook friends see that I know you," Caitlyn typed. After several seconds, the spinning circle ended in a new message.

"Do you really feel that way?" was the simple message Marsha sent.

"Oh my God! Seriously? How stupid are you?" Caitlyn typed. "You're not only the ugliest person I've ever seen in my life, you're the stupidest. YES! I really feel that way! In fact, I wish you would just go kill yourself!"

The reply box remained empty. No spinning circle indicated the conversation would be continuing. There was no way for Caitlyn to top her final insult, so she simply waited for the reaction.

After a few moments passed with nothing happening, Caitlyn walked into the bathroom she shared with her brother. She washed her face, brushed her teeth, and combed her hair. When she returned to her room, there was still nothing but radio silence from Marsha Manson.

Caitlyn opened a new message box to send the promised link to Andromeda. Just as she was copying and pasting the hyperlink into the new screen, she was startled by her mother's scream. Caitlyn pushed her chair away from the computer and ran from her room into the hall. Her father was rounding the opposite corner and they met at the doorway to Marshall's room. The door stood open with the master key protruding from the lock.

She could hear her mother screaming "Help me get him down! Help me get him down!" in the background, but Caitlyn was frozen. She could see her brother's high-heeled feet and the black dress he was wearing through her mother's arms. Caitlyn's father pushed past her to lift Marshall's hanging body, but it was too late.

She remembered one of her parents, or maybe both of her parents yelling, "Call 911."

She even remembered talking to the dispatcher, but when the ambulance arrived, the paramedics just shook their heads.

There was nothing they could do. Caitlyn tried to tell them there had been a mistake. She tried to explain to the ambulance crew that the messages she sent were meant for someone else. She tried to take it all back.

One word repeated in Caitlyn's mind over and over. *"UNDO! UNDO! UNDO!"*, but the button that would make things alright again didn't exist in real life.

She watched as her father removed the leather belt from his son's neck. She watched as he cradled her brother's head and sobbed.

"undo."

About the Author

Coleen Liebsch began writing in middle-school. With the encouragement of her English  teacher, and now editor, Deborah Merkwan, Coleen decided to pursue writing as a career.

Eight years later she has nine of her own books published. She also owns PS Publishing and is the founder and CEO of the Books 4 Kids Program.

For more information about Coleen and the other authors of PS Publishing, visit

www.PublishPS.com.

Did you enjoy this book? If so, please leave a review and comment on Amazon!

www.ingramcontent.com/pod-product-compliance
Lightning Source LLC
Chambersburg PA
CBHW070454170726
48291CB00005B/1745